A Splendid Friend, Indeed

Suzanne Bloom

SCHOLASTIC INC.

New York Toronto London Auckland Sydney
Mexico City New Delhi Hong Kong Buenos Aires

ISBN 0-439-85848-8

Text and illustrations copyright © 2005 by Suzanne Bloom.
All rights reserved. Published by Scholastic Inc., 557 Broadway,
New York, NY 10012, by arrangement with Boyds Mills Press.
SCHOLASTIC and associated logos are trademarks
and/or registered trademarks of Scholastic Inc.

12 11 10 9 8 7 6 5 4 3 2 1   6 7 8 9 10 11/0

Printed in the U.S.A.   08

First Scholastic printing, February 2006

The text is set in 42-point Optima.

The illustrations are done in pastel.

To R. H. B.,
my dad

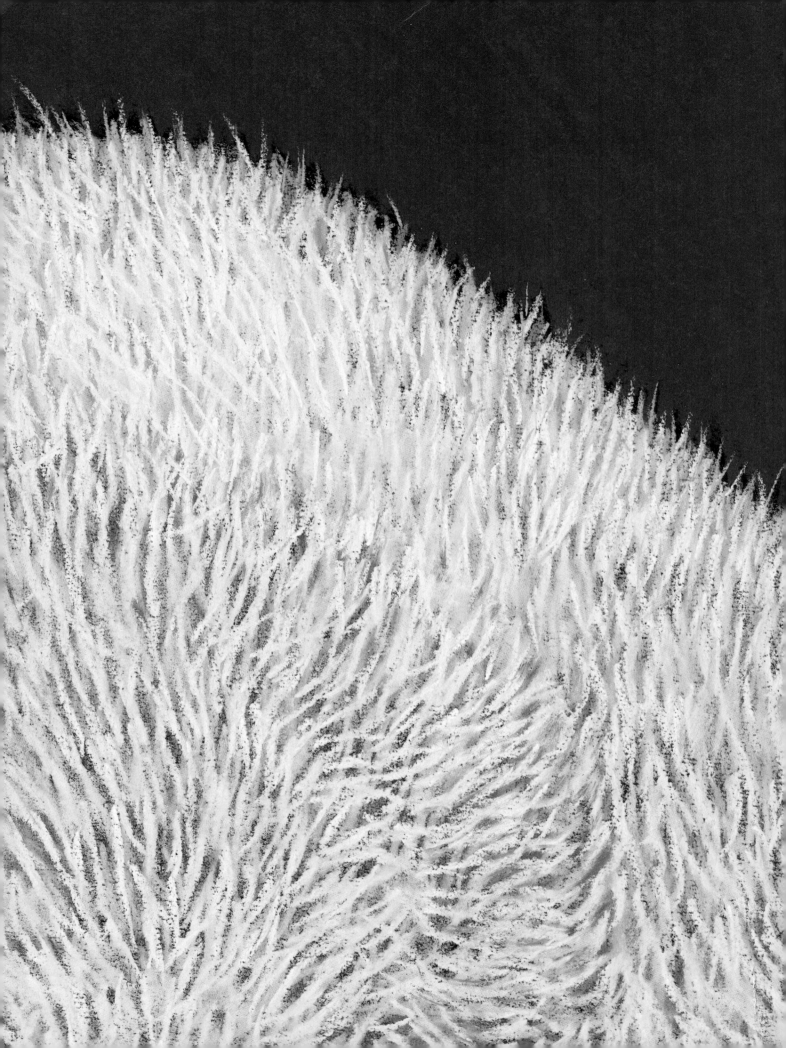

What are you doing?
Are you reading?

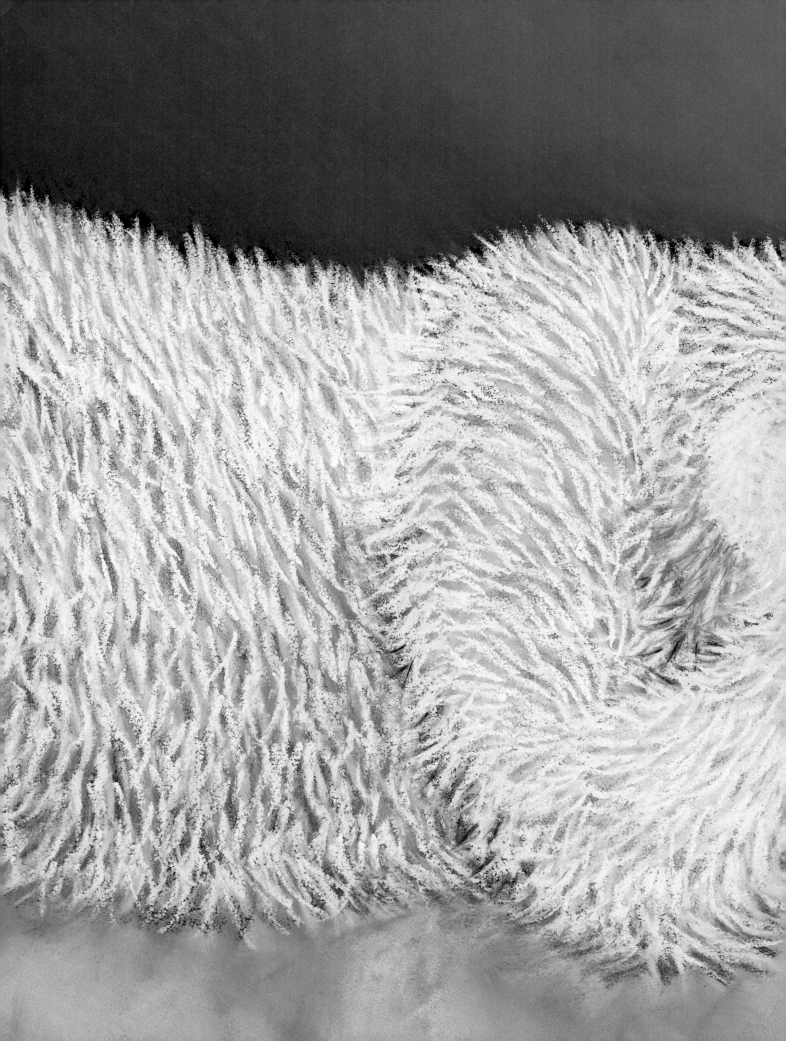

I like to read.

Do you want to hear me read?

Now what are you doing?
Writing?

I like to write.

Do you want to
see me write?

What are you doing now?
Thinking?

Thinking makes me hungry.
Are you hungry?
I think I'll go make a snack.

I'm back.
I made a snack.

I wrote a note.
I'll read it to you.

I like you.
Indeed I do.
You are my splendid friend.

Thank you.
I like you, too.
Indeed, I do.

You are my splendid friend.
My splendid friend, indeed.